DELPHIN! SEND PALAEMON AND HIS LEGION OF SHARKS TO THE WESTERN FRONT! WE MUST *NEUTRALIZE* THOSE *LEVIATHANS!*

YES, LORD!

HELLO, PERCY.

...DAD?

WHERE ARE YOUR SHORTS AND HAWAIIAN SHIRT? WHY ARE YOU SO...

OLD?

THE *WAR* HAS BEEN HARD ON ME.

I AM IMMORTAL, BUT I REFLECT THE STATE OF MY REALM. AND RIGHT NOW, THAT STATE IS *GRIM.*

THE BATTLE AGAINST *OCEANUS* GOES...POORLY.

OCEANUS? THE *TITAN* OF THE SEA?

INDEED. HE WAS NEUTRAL IN THE FIRST WAR OF THE GODS AND TITANS. BUT KRONOS HAS CONVINCED HIM TO FIGHT.

IT IS NOT A GOOD SIGN. HE WOULD NOT COMMIT UNLESS HE WAS *CERTAIN* HE COULD PICK THE WINNING SIDE.

EVEN WITH MIGHTY *BRIARES* FIGHTING FOR US, HE IS ONE AGAINST MANY.

LONG ISLAND, NEW YORK.

CAMP HALF-BLOOD.

HIDDEN REFUGE FOR THE CHILDREN OF GREEK GODS AND HUMANS.

PERCY!

YOU MADE IT!

WAIT...WHERE'S BECKENDORF?

OH, NO...

"...POOR SILENA."

NO.

NO. *NO.*

I'M SURE YOU DID EVERYTHING YOU COULD, PERCY.

I'M GLAD YOU'RE NOT DEAD, SEAWEED BRAIN.

THANKS. ME, TOO.

CHIRON, I SAW MY DAD. HIS KINGDOM IS UNDER ATTACK FROM OCEANUS. BUT HE MADE ME LEAVE ANYWAY.

HE SAID TO TELL YOU IT'S TIME. I NEED TO KNOW THE *FULL PROPHECY.*

I'VE DREADED THIS DAY.

VERY WELL. I WILL CONVENE A WAR COUNCIL.

THERE ARE *MANY MATTERS* TO DISCUSS.

ANNABETH WILL TAKE YOU TO LEARN THE TRUTH-- *ALL* OF IT.

"GO AND SEE THE *ORACLE*."

THIS IS MY FOURTH TIME UP HERE. I NEVER UNDERSTOOD THIS.

WHY DOES THE ORACLE HAVE TO BE A *MUMMY*?

SHE WASN'T ALWAYS A MUMMY. FOR *THOUSANDS OF YEARS* THE SPIRIT OF THE ORACLE LIVED INSIDE A BEAUTIFUL MAIDEN. IT WAS PASSED DOWN FROM GENERATION TO GENERATION.

CHIRON TOLD ME *SHE* WAS LIKE THAT FIFTY YEARS AGO. BUT SHE WAS THE LAST.

SO NOW WHAT? USUALLY THERE'S GREEN MIST AND THINGS GET EVEN *CREEPIER*. THE WHOLE OUT-OF-BODY VOICE THING.

O ORACLE, THE TIME IS AT HAND. I ASK FOR THE *GREAT PROPHECY*.

THANKS.

THE BIG MYSTERY OF MY LIFE WAS HANGING AROUND HER NECK THE WHOLE TIME?!

LET'S GET TO THE WAR COUNCIL.

PERCY. YOU NEED TO KNOW.

READ.

"A HALF-BLOOD OF THE ELDEST GODS...

...SHALL REACH SIXTEEN AGAINST ALL ODDS...

"AND SEE THE WORLD IN ENDLESS SLEEP...

"...THE HERO'S SOUL, CURSED BLADE SHALL REAP...

"A SINGLE CHOICE...

"...A SINGLE CHOICE SHALL END HIS DAYS...OLYMPUS TO PRESERVE OR RAZE."

YOU SEE NOW, PERCY, WHY WE THOUGHT IT BEST NOT TO TELL YOU THE WHOLE PROPHECY. YOU'VE HAD ENOUGH ON YOUR SHOULDERS.

WITHOUT REALIZING I WAS GOING TO *DIE* IN THE END ANYWAY?

YEAH, I GET IT.

YOU NEED TO THINK ABOUT THIS. YOU NEED TIME.

NO. IF I DIE, I DIE. I CAN'T WORRY ABOUT THAT, RIGHT?

YOU DON'T MEAN THAT, PERCY.

WE HAVE BIGGER PROBLEMS. THERE'S A *SPY* IN CAMP. KRONOS KNEW WE WERE COMING TO BOMB THE *PRINCESS ANDROMEDA*.

HE WAS *WAITING*.

A *SPY?*

WHO?

IT MAKES SENSE. SOMEONE HAS BEEN FEEDING INFORMATION TO LUKE FOR YEARS. AND I'M AFRAID OUR PROBLEMS ARE EVEN LARGER STILL.

TYPHON HAS RETURNED.

"THE MOST *HORRIBLE* MONSTER OF ALL. THE BIGGEST SINGLE THREAT THE GODS *EVER* FACED.

"HE HAS BEEN FREED FROM HIS *PRISON* UNDER MOUNT ST. HELENS AT LAST."

THE GODS HAVE BEEN FIGHTING *M* FOR DAYS, TRYING TO SLOW DOWN. BUT TYPHON MARCHES *RWARD*. TOWARD NEW YORK.

"TOWARD *OLYMPUS*."

TYPHON WILL ARRIVE IN FIVE DAYS.

FIVE DAYS? HAT'S THE AY I TURN SIXTEEN.

WELL, I THINK THAT'S QUITE *ENOUGH* FOR ONE COUNCIL.

NIGHT HAS FALLEN.

"WE HAVE A *BURIAL SHROUD* TO BURN."

HAIL, *CHARLES BECKENDORF*, SON OF HEPHAESTUS, WHO FELL *HONORABLY* IN BATTLE AGAINST THE FORCES OF THE TITAN LORD.

HAIL!

IT'S ALL MY FAULT....

DON'T SAY THAT, SILENA. BECKENDORF SACRIFICED HIMSELF FOR THE GOOD OF THE WAR. EVEN *ARES* WOULD BE PROUD.

BECKENDORF WAS GOING TO COLLEGE AFTER THE SUMMER. HE AND SILENA WERE SO HAPPY TOGETHER.

NOW HE'S JUST... *GONE*.

IT KIND OF MAKES YOU THINK. ABOUT...WHAT'S IMPORTANT.

ABOUT LOSING PEOPLE WHO ARE IMPORTANT.

ANNABETH, I...

I, UM, HAD THIS VISION OF RACHEL. RIGHT AFTER THE *PRINCESS ANDROMEDA* EXPLODED.

RACHEL? YOU'RE TALKING TO ME RIGHT NOW ABOUT *RACHEL?*

IT'S JUST...SHE SAYS THERE'S SOMETHING SHE HAS TO TELL ME. WHAT IF SHE KNOWS SOMETHING ABOUT THE *WAR?*

ABOUT WHAT KRONOS IS PLANNING? YOU KNOW HOW SHE CAN SEE THINGS.

WE'LL JUST HAVE TO BE READY.

HOW? THE ARES AND APOLLO CABINS CAN'T EVEN STOP FIGHTING *EACH OTHER*.

YOU'RE THE BEST STRATEGIST I KNOW. IF YOU WERE KRONOS, WHAT WOULD YOU DO NEXT?

I'D USE *TYPHON* AS A DISTRACTION.

THEN I'D HIT *OLYMPUS* DIRECTLY, WHILE THE GODS WERE IN THE WEST.

MEANWHILE, HALF OUR CAMP HAS DEFECTED TO THE OTHER SIDE. AND THERE'S NO WORD FROM *GROVER* SINCE HE LEFT FOR CENTRAL PARK MONTHS AGO. WE'RE GOING TO NEED HIM AND THE POWER OF THE *WILD* TO GET THROUGH THIS.

ON THE *PLUS* SIDE, I'M SUPPOSED TO GET MY *DUMB SOUL* REAPED. SO AFTER KRONOS WINS, AT LEAST I WON'T BE AROUND TO *ANNOY* YOU ANYMORE.

YOU REALLY ARE *STUPID*, YOU KNOW THAT, SEAWEED BRAIN?

YEAH. I KNOW.

I ALWAYS LIKED HIM.

NICO?

I TALKED TO HIS *GHOST* IN THE UNDERWORLD. HE DOESN'T BLAME YOU. HE FIGURED YOU'D BE BEATING YOURSELF UP, AND HE SAID YOU SHOULDN'T.

IT'S NOT THAT EASY.

THAT DOESN'T MATTER NOW.

TYPHON IS HEADED THIS WAY. MOST OF THE OTHER TITANS ARE UNLEASHED. THIS CAMP IS *NO MATCH* FOR THEIR ARMY, AND YOU KNOW IT.

THIS COMES DOWN TO YOU AND LUKE. AND THERE'S ONLY *ONE WAY* YOU CAN BEAT LUKE, NOW THAT *KRONOS* HAS TAKEN HIM OVER.

TWO YEARS AGO, MY SISTER GAVE HER LIFE TO PROTECT YOU. I WANT YOU TO HONOR THAT. DO WHATEVER IT TAKES TO STAY ALIVE AND *DEFEAT* KRONOS.

PERCY. YOU *KNOW* WHAT YOU HAVE TO CHOOSE.

ALL RIGHT. WHAT DO WE DO FIRST?

WESTPORT, CONNECTICUT.

WHERE'S MRS. O'LEARY?

I LEFT HER SNORING IN THE WOODS.

THIS IS WHERE LUKE IS FROM? WHAT ARE WE SUPPOSED TO DO HERE?

RING THE DOORBELL.

DING DONG

LUKE!

I *TOLD* THEM YOU WOULD COME *HOME!* I *KNEW* IT!

OH, MY *DEAR BOY.* COME IN. I HAVE YOUR LUNCH READY. PEANUT BUTTER AND JELLY SANDWICHES, COOKIES, AND KOOL-AID. YOUR *FAVORITE.*

SIT DOWN, SIT DOWN. I WAS JUST ABOUT TO TAKE THE COOKIES OUT OF THE OVEN.

UM, MS. CASTELLAN?

WE NEED TO ASK YOU ABOUT YOUR *SON.*

THEY TOLD ME HE WOULD NEVER COME HOME. BUT *I* KNEW BETTER. HE WAS SO YOUNG WHEN HE LEFT. THIRD GRADE. THAT'S *TOO YOUNG* TO RUN AWAY.

HE SAID HE'D BE BACK FOR LUNCH. I'VE BEEN WAITING. HE'LL BE BACK VERY SOON.

WHY, LUKE, *THERE* YOU ARE! YOU LOOK SO HANDSOME. YOU HAVE YOUR *FATHER'S* EYES.

SUCH A GOOD MAN. HE COMES TO *VISIT* ME, YOU KNOW.

...MS. CASTELLAN?

CALL ME *MOM,* DEAR.

HAVE YOU SEEN LUKE SINCE HE LEFT HOME?

WELL, OF COURSE!

IT WAS... OH, GOODNESS... THE LAST TIME, HE LOOKED SO *DIFFERENT*.

A SCAR. A TERRIBLE SCAR, AND HIS VOICE FULL OF *PAIN*...

HE WAS GOING TO A *RIVER*. HE SAID HE NEEDED MY BLESSING, AND I GAVE IT TO HIM...OF COURSE I DID.

AHHHH!

MS. CASTELLAN?

MY CHILD. HERMES, HELP! MUST PROTECT HIM.

NOT HIS FATE!

NOT HIS FATE!

...LUKE?

DEAR ME. I'VE ALWAYS BEEN ABLE TO SEE THROUGH THE *MIST*. THEY OFFERED ME AN IMPORTANT JOB. YOUR FATHER *WARNED* ME NOT TO TRY.

BUT I HAD TO. IT WAS MY *DESTINY*. I STILL CAN'T GET THE IMAGES OUT OF MY HEAD. THEY MAKE EVERYTHING SEEM SO FUZZY.

GODDESS? LL JUST, YOU NOW, PUT MY WORD AWAY NOW.

MY LADY. WHY AREN'T YOU WITH THE OTHER OLYMPIANS, FIGHTING TYPHON?

I'M NOT MUCH FOR FIGHTING. BESIDES, SOMEONE HAS TO KEEP THE **HOME FIRES** BURNING WHILE THE OTHER GODS ARE AWAY.

SO, YOU'RE GUARDING **MOUNT OLYMPUS?**

"GUARD" MAY BE TOO STRONG A WORD. BUT IF YOU EVER NEED A WARM PLACE TO SIT AND A HOME-COOKED MEAL, YOU ARE WELCOME TO VISIT.

NOW EAT. TELL ME OF YOUR VISIT WITH **MAY CASTELLAN.**

ONE MINUTE SHE WAS ALL HAPPY. AND THEN SHE WAS **FREAKING OUT** ABOUT HER SON'S FATE, LIKE SHE KNEW HE'D TURNED INTO KRONOS.

IT IS A STORY I DO NOT LIKE TO TELL, BUT MAY CASTELLAN HAD THE **GIFT** OF **SIGHT.** SHE ATTRACTED THE ATTENTION OF HERMES, AND THEY HAD A BEAUTIFUL BABY BOY. FOR A WHILE THEY WERE HAPPY...

...AND THEN SHE WENT **TOO FAR.**

I TELL YOU THIS BECAUSE TO UNDERSTAND YOUR ENEMY LUKE, YOU MUST UNDERSTAND HIS **FAMILY.**

WILL YOU FOLLOW LUKE'S PATH? SEEK THE SAME POWERS?

WE HAVE NO CHOICE, MY LADY. IT'S THE **ONLY** WAY PERCY STANDS A CHANCE.

HMMM.

YOU ARE A GOOD HERO, PERCY JACKSON. NOT TOO PROUD. I LIKE THAT. BUT YOU HAVE MUCH TO LEARN. NOT **ALL** POWERS ARE SPECTACULAR.

WHEN DIONYSUS WAS MADE A GOD, I GAVE UP MY THRONE FOR HIM. IT WAS THE ONLY WAY TO AVOID **CIVIL WAR** AMONG THE GODS.

NOW I TEND THE FIRE. NO ONE WILL EVER WRITE EPIC POEMS ABOUT THE DEEDS OF HESTIA. BUT THAT IS NO MATTER. I KEEP THE **PEACE.**

"NOW I RETURN YOU TO YOUR **OWN** HEARTH."

HEY, MOM.

AAAAAA!

WHY ARE YOU UP SO LATE?

...PERCY?

PERCY!

GROVER!

GROVER! WE NEED YOU!

PERCY, WE DON'T HAVE TIME TO STAND AROUND--

WAIT FOR IT....

RSSTLE

RSSTLE

WHUMMP

≥YAWN≥

UNCLE FERDINAND? IS IT *BREAKFAST TIME* YET?

GOOD TO SEE YOU, G-MAN. YOU REMEMBER NICO.

PERCY! I MISSED YOU! I MISS CAMP!

TRY *CHECKING IN* ONCE IN A WHILE. WE'VE ALL BEEN WORRIED ABOUT YOU. WHERE'VE YOU BEEN THE LAST TWO MONTHS?

TWO MONTHS?!

I HAVEN'T--

I...I REMEMBER NOW.

I WAS SEARCHING THE WOODS, AND I FELT THIS TREMBLE IN THE GROUND, LIKE SOMETHING *POWERFUL* WAS NEAR.

I TRACKED IT TO THE PARK, WHERE THIS MAN IN A LONG BLACK COAT WAS WALKING. NO SHADOW. HE KIND OF *SHIMMERED* AS HE MOVED.

LIKE A MIRAGE?

JUST LIKE THAT. HE WAS LOOKING AT ALL THE BUILDINGS. SAID SOMETHING ABOUT *"MAKING ESTIMATES."*

I TOLD HIM THE PARK WAS UNDER MY PROTECTION, AND HE JUST LAUGHED. HE SAID I WAS LUCKY HE WAS SAVING HIS STRENGTH FOR THE *MAIN EVENT*. THEN HE TOLD ME, "PLEASANT DREAMS."

PERCY, MEET ACHILLES.

LIKE, *THE* ACHILLES?

DO NOT DO THIS. IT WILL MAKE YOU POWERFUL. BUT IT WILL ALSO MAKE YOU WEAK.

YOUR PROWESS IN COMBAT WILL BE *BEYOND* ANY MORTAL'S, BUT YOUR WEAKNESSES-- YOUR *FAILINGS*--WILL INCREASE AS WELL.

I HAVE TO. OTHERWISE I DON'T STAND A CHANCE.

THIS IS HOW LUKE PREPARED HIMSELF TO HOST THE SPIRIT OF KRONOS WITHOUT HIS BODY DISINTEGRATING. HE'S TAKEN ON THE POWERS GRANTED TO *YOU* WHEN YOU BATHED IN THE RIVER STYX.

HE'S *INVINCIBLE*.

LET THE GODS WITNESS I TRIED.

CONCENTRATE ON YOUR *MORTAL POINT*, ONE SPOT THAT WILL REMAIN VULNERABLE. THIS IS THE POINT WHERE YOUR SOUL WILL *ANCHOR* YOUR BODY TO THE MORTAL WORLD.

LOSE SIGHT OF IT, AND THE STYX WILL BURN YOU TO ASHES.

WHETHER YOU SURVIVE THIS OR NOT, YOU HAVE SEALED YOUR DOOM.

UHNNNN

EMPIRE STATE

FORTY **DEMIGODS** ATTRACT AN AWFUL LOT OF MONSTERS. YOU REALLY WANT US HANGING OUT IN YOUR LOBBY?

H-HAVE IT YOUR WAY, KID. ELEVATOR ON THE RIGHT.

THANKS. I KNOW THE WAY.

WHAT'S YOUR NAME, KIDDO?

A-ANNABETH.

TELL YOU WHAT, ANNABETH-- YOU'RE PRETTY FIERCE. WE COULD USE A FIGHTER LIKE YOU.

HOW'D YOU LIKE A *REAL* MONSTER-SLAYING WEAPON? THIS IS CELESTIAL BRONZE. WORKS A LOT BETTER THAN A HAMMER.

YOU'RE NOT GOING TO TAKE ME BACK TO MY FAMILY, ARE YOU?

THEY DON'T WANT ME. I RAN AWAY.

IT TAKES A *CLEVER WARRIOR* TO USE A KNIFE. I HAVE A FEELING YOU'RE PRETTY CLEVER.

YOU'RE PART OF *OUR* FAMILY NOW. AND I PROMISE I WON'T LET ANYTHING HURT YOU.

I WON'T *FAIL* YOU LIKE OUR FAMILIES DID US. DEAL?

DEAL!

UHNNNN

PERCY? WHAT'S WRONG?

DID... DID YOU SEE THAT?

HOW LONG WAS I OUT?

YOU WEREN'T OUT AT ALL.

YOU LOOKED AT HESTIA FOR LIKE *ONE SECOND* AND COLLAPSED.

UM, LADY HESTIA, WE'VE COME ON *URGENT BUSINESS.* WE NEED TO SEE--

WE *KNOW* WHAT YOU NEED.

LORD HERMES, KRONOS IS GOING TO ATTACK NEW YORK.

YOU MUST SUSPECT THAT. ASK ZEUS TO SEND SOME OF THE GODS BACK TO DEFEND THE CITY.

ANNABETH CHASE. *ATHENA* KNEW YOU WOULD COME HERE. SHE, TOO, THINKS THE BATTLE AGAINST TYPHON IS A *RUSE* MEANT TO DRAW US AWAY FROM OLYMPUS.

YOU AND YOUR MOTHER SEEM TO FORGET THAT TYPHON NEARLY DESTROYED US AGES AGO. HE IS OUR *GREATEST ENEMY.* WE GODS NEED *ALL* OUR POWER TO DEFEAT HIM.

THE DEMIGODS MUST DEFEND MANHATTAN ALONE.

PERCY, ATHENA TOLD ME TO CONVEY A *MESSAGE* TO YOU. "REMEMBER THE RIVERS."

I MUST RETURN NOW. I HAVE A *WAR* TO FIGHT.

LORD HERMES. I...

...I WANTED TO SAY... I'M SORRY.

ABOUT LUKE.

BETTER THAT YOU HAD LEFT THAT SUBJECT *ALONE.*

YOU SHOULD HAVE SAVED HIM WHEN YOU HAD THE CHANCE. YOU ARE THE *ONLY* ONE WHO COULD.

ANNABETH, IT'S NOT YOUR FAULT. HERMES PROBABLY FEELS GUILTY ABOUT LUKE AND HE'S LOOKING FOR SOMEBODY TO BLAME. YOU DIDN'T DO ANYTHING WRONG.

RIGHT?

HESTIA MENTIONED THE CURSE OF ACHILLES. DID YOU...

...DID YOU BATHE IN THE *RIVER STYX*?

UM, IT WAS MORE LIKE A SHORT SWIM.

DO YOU HAVE ANY IDEA HOW *DANGEROUS* THAT WAS?

I HAD NO CHOICE. IT'S THE *ONLY WAY* I CAN STAND UP TO LUKE.

DI IMMORTALES, OF COURSE! THAT'S WHY LUKE DIDN'T DIE WHEN KRONOS *POSSESSED* HIM.

HE WENT TO THE STYX...

OH NO, LUKE. WHAT WERE YOU *THINKING*?

SO NOW YOU'RE WORRIED ABOUT *LUKE* AGAIN. GREAT.

WHAT?

FORGET IT.

PERCY! ANNABETH! YOU NEED TO SEE THIS.

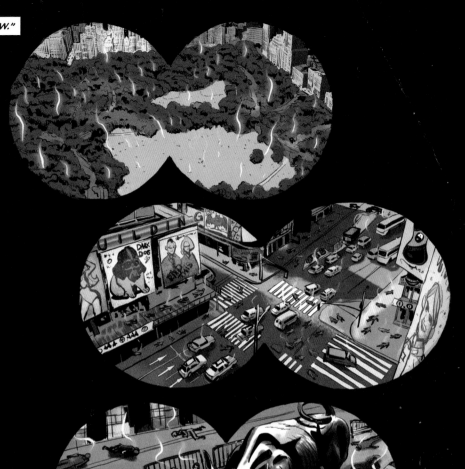

IS EVERYONE... DEAD?

NOT DEAD. *MORPHEUS.* HE TOLD GROVER HE WAS SAVING HIS ENERGY FOR THE MAIN EVENT.

HE'S PUT THE *ENTIRE ISLAND* OF MANHATTAN TO SLEEP, JUST LIKE THE PROPHECY SAID.

"AND SEE THE WORLD IN *ENDLESS SLEEP.*"

MORE MONSTERS MARCHING THROUGH THE *TUNNELS!*

WHICH TUNNELS?

...*ALL* OF THEM.

EACH CABIN, TAKE A TUNNEL. IT DOESN'T MATTER HOW MANY MONSTERS COME AT YOU. YOU ARE THE *GREATEST HEROES* OF THIS MILLENNIUM.

FIGHT BRAVELY, AND WE WILL WIN.

FOR OLYMPUS!

FOR OLYMPUS!

FOR OLYMPUS!

ANNABETH, MEET ME BACK IN MANHATTAN. BATTERY PARK.

WHAT ARE YOU GOING TO DO?

HMPH. YOU'VE STOPPED NOTHING, JACKSON. MERELY DELAYED THE INEVITABLE.

UNTIL THIS EVENING.

MEDICS!

PLAZA HOTEL.

CURRENT HOME BASE TO CAMP HALF-BLOOD'S BATTLE INFIRMARY.

ANNABETH...

THE HEALERS FROM THE APOLLO CABIN SAY YOU'LL BE OKAY. THE POISON HADN'T GOTTEN PAST YOUR SHOULDER YET.

THIS IS ALL *MY* FAULT. I'VE NEVER BEEN ANY GOOD AT CAMP. NOT LIKE YOU TWO.

IF I WAS A BETTER FIGHTER...

NO, SILENA, HOW COULD IT BE YOUR FAULT?

YOU'RE A GREAT CAMPER. YOU'RE THE BEST PEGASUS RIDER WE HAVE. AND YOU GET ALONG WITH PEOPLE.

BELIEVE ME, ANYONE WHO CAN MAKE FRIENDS WITH *CLARISSE* HAS TALENT.

THAT'S IT! WE NEED THE *ARES* CABIN. I CAN TALK TO CLARISSE. I *KNOW* I CAN CONVINCE HER TO HELP US.

I WON'T LET YOU DOWN PERCY!

YOU'RE CUTE WHEN YOU'RE WORRIED.

WHY DID YOU TAKE THAT ARROW?

YOU WOULD'VE DONE THE SAME FOR ME.

MY *ACHILLES SPOT*. IT'S ON MY BACK. IF YOU HADN'T TAKEN THAT ARROW, I WOULD'VE DIED.

HOW DID YOU KNOW?

I DON'T KNOW. I JUST HAD THIS FEELING YOU WERE IN DANGER.

THERE'S SOMETHING I NEED TO TELL YOU.

HEY, YOU NEED TO REST--

NO, I *WANT* TO TELL YOU. IT'S BEEN BOTHERING ME FOR A LONG TIME.

LAST YEAR... LUKE CAME TO SEE ME IN SAN FRANCISCO.

HE CAME TO YOUR *HOUSE*?

IN PERSON?

HE CAME UNDER A FLAG OF TRUCE. HE LOOKED *SCARED*. HE TOLD ME KRONOS WAS GOING TO USE HIM TO TAKE OVER THE WORLD.

HE SAID HE WANTED TO RUN AWAY, LIKE THE OLD DAYS. HE WANTED *ME* TO COME WITH HIM.

HERMES WAS RIGHT. MAYBE IF I'D GONE WITH LUKE, I COULD'VE CHANGED HIS MIND. OR...I HAD MY DAGGER. LUKE WAS *UNARMED*. I COULD'VE...

LUKE SAID KRONOS WOULD USE HIM LIKE A *STEPPING-STONE*. WHAT IF KRONOS HAS A PLAN TO BECOME MORE POWERFUL?

I COULD'VE STOPPED HIM. THIS *WHOLE WAR* IS MY FAULT.

IT'S OKAY. YOU KNOW KILLING LUKE WOULDN'T HAVE BEEN RIGHT.

DON'T WORRY ABOUT IT NOW.

PERCY? *GROVER* IS HERE. YOU SHOULD HEAR WHAT HE HAS TO SAY.

I HEARD ABOUT ANNABETH. IS SHE...?

SHE'S GOING TO BE FINE. SHE'S RESTING.

SO WHAT'S UP?

I DID WHAT YOU SAID. I COLLECTED FORCES AND WENT AFTER MORPHEUS.

WE RAN INTO A PACK OF GIANTS AT FORT WASHINGTON. THE RIVER SPIRITS DROWNED THE GIANTS IN THE END, BUT LOSSES WERE HEAVY.

TWENTY SATYRS DIED.

IT GETS WORSE.

THALIA? THE *HUNTERS OF ARTEMIS* ARE HERE?

DIDN'T THINK WE'D MISS THE *FUN*, DID YOU?

WE SEALED OFF THE SUBWAY TUNNELS INTO MANHATTAN, BUT KRONOS'S FORCES ARE STILL GATHERING. I THINK HE'S WAITING FOR A *NIGHT ATTACK*.

MOST OF HIS MONSTERS *ARE* MORE POWERFUL AT NIGHT.

AND THE WAY KRONOS SHOWED UP AT THE WILLIAMSBURG BRIDGE, IT'S LIKE HE KNEW WHERE OUR WEAKEST POINTS WOULD BE.

HIS *SPY* IS STILL SENDING HIM INFORMATION.

THERE'S A SPY?

SOMEONE INSIDE CAMP HALF-BLOOD. IT COULD BE ANY OF US.

BUT WE CAN'T OBSESS ABOUT THAT NOW.

IF WE'RE SUPSICIOUS OF EACH OTHER, WE'LL TEAR OURSELVES APART.

PERCY...THERE'S ONE MORE THING.

ON OUR WAY HERE WE ENCOUNTERED A *TITAN*. HE'S WAITING TO MEET YOU UNDER A FLAG OF TRUCE.

"HE HAS A *MESSAGE* FROM *KRONOS*."

PERCY JACKSON.

IT'S A GREAT HONOR TO MEET YOU.

I AM *PROMETHEUS*.

THE *FIRE-STEALER* GUY? THE CHAINED-TO-THE-ROCK-WITH-THE-*VULTURES* GUY?

YES, I STOLE FIRE FROM THE GODS AND GAVE IT TO YOUR ANCESTORS.

IN RETURN, THE EVER *MERCIFUL* ZEUS HAD ME CHAINED TO A ROCK TO BE *TORTURED* FOR ALL ETERNITY.

HERCULES FREED ME. SO YOU SEE, I HAVE A SOFT SPOT FOR HEROES. SOME OF YOU CAN BE QUITE CIVILIZED.

THAT'S WHY I'VE COME TO *END* THIS BLOODSHED. PERCY, YOUR POSITION WEAK. YOU KNOW YOU CAN'T STOP ANOTHER ASSAULT.

YEAH? I'LL GIVE *YOU* A DEAL: TELL KRONOS TO CALL OFF HIS ATTACK, LEAVE LUKE'S BODY, AND RETURN TO THE PIT OF TARTARUS.

THEN MAYBE I WON'T HAVE TO *DESTROY* HIM.

YOUR OBSTINANCE IS REGRETTABLE.

IF YOU CHANGE YOUR MIND--

--I HAVE A GIFT FOR YOU.

THIS BELONGED TO MY SISTER-IN-LAW *PANDORA.*

AS IN... *PANDORA'S BOX*?

I DON'T KNOW HOW THIS *BOX* BUSINESS GOT STARTED. IT WAS NEVER A BOX. IT WAS A *PITHOS*-- A STORAGE JAR.

BUT YES, SHE DID OPEN THIS JAR, WHICH CONTAINED MOST OF THE DEMONS THAT *HAUNT* MANKIND TO THIS DAY.

FEAR, DEATH, HUNGER, SICKNESS. ONLY *ONE* SPIRIT REMAINED INSIDE.

HOPE.

VERY GOOD, PERCY. *ELPIS*, THE SPIRIT OF HOPE, WOULD NOT ABANDON HUMANITY.

HOPE DOES NOT LEAVE WITHOUT BEING GIVEN PERMISSION. SHE CAN ONLY BE RELEASED BY A CHILD OF *MAN*.

I GIVE YOU THIS AS A REMINDER OF WHAT THE GODS ARE LIKE. KEEP ELPIS, IF YOU WISH.

BUT IF YOU DECIDE THAT YOU HAVE SEEN ENOUGH DESTRUCTION--ENOUGH *FUTILE SUFFERING*-- THEN OPEN THE JAR. LET ELPIS GO. GIVE UP HOPE, AND I WILL KNOW THAT YOU ARE SURRENDERING.

I PROMISE KRONOS WILL BE LENIENT. HE WILL SPARE THE SURVIVORS.

WHERE ARE YOU GOING? *I DON'T WANT THIS THING!*

TOO LATE. THE GIFT IS GIVEN. IT CANNOT BE TAKEN BACK.

WE WILL SEE YOU AGAIN SOON, PERCY JACKSON.

ONE WAY OR ANOTHER.

WHAT IF PROMETHEUS IS *RIGHT*? WHAT IF THE GODS COULD'VE WARNED LUKE AND STOPPED ALL THIS FROM HAPPENING?

PERCY, YOU CAN'T START FEELING SORRY FOR LUKE. WE ALL HAVE TOUGH THINGS TO DEAL WITH. *ALL* DEMIGODS DO.

OUR PARENTS ARE HARDLY EVER AROUND. BUT LUKE MADE BAD CHOICES. NOBODY FORCED HIM TO TURN SIDES. TO GIVE HIMSELF TO KRONOS.

YOU'RE RIGHT.

GROVER, TAKE THE VASE TO MOUNT OLYMPUS. GIVE IT TO HESTIA.

WHY?

BECAUSE HOPE SURVIVES BEST AT THE HEARTH. WITH HESTIA GUARDING IT, WE WON'T BE TEMPTED TO GIVE IT UP.

IT'LL BE NIGHT SOON, THALIA.

MAYBE OUR *LAST* NIGHT.

ROUND UP EVERY WARRIOR WE HAVE. WE'LL MAKE OUR STAND AT *CENTRAL PARK*.

THANK THE GODS, CHIRON AND THE PARTY PONIES ARRIVED TO DO THEIR PART.

AND ANOTHER DAWN BROKE WITH OUR HEROES SURVIVING THE NIGHT.

BARELY.

THANKS FOR HELPING OUT, CHIRON. KRONOS'S ARMY PUSHED US ALL THE WAY BACK TO THE EMPIRE STATE BUILDING.

WITHOUT YOU AND THE CENTAURS, I DON'T THINK WE WOULD'VE HELD.

THEN WHAT CHANCE DO WE HAVE? WE CAN'T HOLD OUT FOR ANOTHER DAY.

WE'LL *HAVE* TO.

I'LL SEE ABOUT SETTING SOME NEW TRAPS AROUND THE PERIMETER.

TIME IS SHORT. AS SOON AS KRONOS REGROUPS, HE WILL ATTACK AGAIN. WE WON'T HAVE THE ELEMENT OF SURPRISE ON OUR SIDE.

AND *TYPHON* MARCHES EVER CLOSER. THE GODS HAVE SLOWED HIS APPROACH, BUT HE CANNOT BE STOPPED. ONCE HE AND KRONOS *COMBINE* FORCES...

I WILL HELP. AND MAKE SURE MY BRETHREN DO NOT GET INTO ANY STOCKS OF *ROOT BEER*.

DRINK TOO MUCH OF THAT, AND THEY WILL BE POSITIVELY *USELESS*.

ANNABETH? YOU OKAY?

YOU'RE RIGHT. DUMB QUESTION.

LISTEN... THERE WERE SOME... SOME *VISIONS* HESTIA SHOWED ME. YOU AND THALIA AND LUKE. THE FIRST TIME YOU MET.

LUKE PROMISED HE'D NEVER LET ME GET HURT. HE SAID... HE SAID WE'D BE A NEW FAMILY, AND IT WOULD TURN OUT *BETTER* THAN HIS.

I THOUGHT I'D FOUND A PLACE TO BELONG, BUT IT FELL APART SO FAST. I *HATE* IT WHEN PEOPLE LET ME DOWN. WHEN THINGS ARE TEMPORARY.

I THINK THAT'S WHY I WANT TO BE AN ARCHITECT. TO BUILD THINGS THAT ARE *PERMANENT*.

WHAT IF LUKE IS STILL *FIGHTING*, PERCY? WHAT IF HE'S TRYING TO *RESIST* KRONOS SOMEHOW?

HE COULD STILL BE DOING THAT, RIGHT?

I GUESS I UNDERSTAND WHY YOU WANT TO THINK THAT.

BUT THALIA IS RIGHT. LUKE HAS ALREADY BETRAYED YOU SO MANY TIMES. HE WAS EVIL EVEN *BEFORE* KRONOS POSSESSED HIM.

I DON'T WANT HIM TO HURT YOU ANYMORE.

AND YOU'LL UNDERSTAND IF I KEEP HOPING THERE'S A CHANCE YOU'RE *WRONG*.

DO YOU HEAR THAT?

WHUP WHUP WHUP

WHUP WHUP WHUP WHUP

PERCY! UP HERE!

...RACHEL?

WHAT'S *SHE* DOING HERE?

YOU...YOU SAVED MY LIFE.

YEAH, WELL, LET'S NOT MAKE A HABIT OF IT.

YOU CAN *FLY* A *HELICOPTER*?!

I GUESS SO. NEVER REALLY TRIED BEFORE.

BUT YOU KNOW HOW MY DAD IS CRAZY INTO AVIATION. I TOOK M BEST GUESS AT THE CONTROLS.

WHAT ARE YOU *DOING* HERE, DARE? DON'T YOU KNOW BETTER THAN TO FLY INTO A *WAR ZONE*?

I MADE A DEAL WITH MY DAD TO LOAN ME HIS CORPORATE HELICOPTER.

I HAD TO BE HERE. I KNEW PERCY WAS IN TROUBLE. I'VE BEEN *SEEING* THINGS.

AND I DON'T JUST MEAN HOW I CAN SEE MONSTERS. THIS IS DIFFERENT. I'M SEEING IMAGES. LINES OF TEXT.

THERE'S A *MESSAGE* I HAVE TO GIVE YOU. I CAN'T GET IT OUT OF MY HEAD.

"PERSEUS, YOU ARE NOT THE HERO."

YOU HAVE *INTERESTING INSIGHTS*, RACHEL DARE.

NOT THE HERO OF THE *GREAT PROPHECY*? NOT THE HERO WHO'LL *DEFEAT KRONOS*?

WHAT DO YOU MEAN?

I'M...I'M SORRY, PERCY. THAT'S ALL I KNOW. I HAD TO TELL YOU *BECAUSE--*

OH, NO.

NO, NO, NO...

IT'S LIKE RAC... SAID.

SILENA... ...WHAT DID YOU DO?

"A TRICK THAT ENDS IN DEATH."

WOULDN'T LISTEN...CABIN WOULD... ONLY FOLLOW YOU.

SO YOU STOLE MY ARMOR. YOU WAITED UNTIL CHRIS AND I WENT OUT ON PATROL. YOU STOLE MY ARMOR AND *PRETENDED* TO BE *ME*.

AND NONE OF YOU NOTICED?

DON'T BLAME THEM... THEY WANTED TO... TO BELIEVE I WAS YOU.

ALL MY FAULT...THE DRAKON, CHARLIE'S DEATH...CAMP ENDANGERED...

YOU'RE KRONOS'S SPY.

JACKSON, I WILL GUT YOU IF YOU EVER SAY THAT AGAIN.

BEFORE... BEFORE I LIKED CHARLIE, LUKE WAS NICE TO ME. SO... CHARMING. LATER, I WANTED TO STOP HELPING HIM... BUT HE THREATENED TO TELL...

...HE PROMISED I WAS SAVING LIVES. FEWER PEOPLE...WOULD GET HURT. HE LIED TO ME. HE TOLD ME...HE SAID HE WOULDN'T HURT CHARLIE.

CHARLIE?

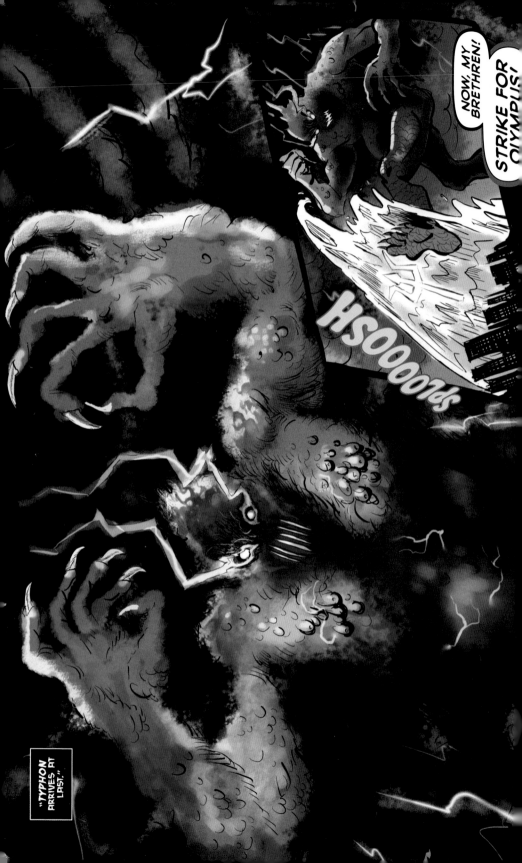

GREEARRRGH!

FWAKKASSH

IT'S...

...IT'S OVER.

WE NEED A BURIAL SHROUD FOR *LUKE CASTELLAN*, SON OF HERMES.

THAT BRINGS US TO THE MATTER OF *THANKING* OUR YOUNG DEMIGOD HEROES.

THALIA GRACE. YOU LED THE HUNTERS OF ARTEMIS WITH *DISTINCTION.* MANY WERE LOST, AND I WILL AID YOU MYSELF IN REFILLING THEIR RANKS.

ALL WHO FELL WILL NEVER BE FORGOTTEN. THEY WILL ACHIEVE *ELYSIUM.*

THANK YOU, FATHER.

TYSON, SON OF POSEIDON. FOR YOUR *BRAVERY* IN WAR, YOU ARE APPOINTED A GENERAL IN THE ARMIES OF OLYMPUS.

YOU SHALL HENCEFORTH LEAD YOUR *CYCLOPS BRETHREN* INTO BATTLE WHENEVER REQUIRED BY THE GODS.

HOORAY!

GROVER UNDERWOOD. FOR YOUR BRAVERY AND SACRIFICE, YOU ARE APPOINTED TO THE COUNCIL OF CLOVEN ELDERS.

ALL SATYRS AND NATURE SPIRITS WILL HENCEFORTH TREAT YOU AS *LORD OF THE WILD.*

UM... REALLY?

NICO DI ANGELO, YOU RISKED MUCH.

FOR GUIDING PERCY AND SHOWING THE FORESIGHT TO UNDERSTAND THAT THE WORLD OF THE LIVING COULD NOT SURVIVE WITHOUT THE *REALM* OF THE *DEAD*--

IF IT'S ALL THE SAME, ZEUS, DAD AND I WILL WORK IT OUT. *TOGETHER.*

ANNABETH CHASE. YOU HAVE EXCEEDED *ALL* EXPECTATIONS. YOUR WITS, YOUR STRENGTH, AND YOUR COURAGE MADE OUR VICTORY POSSIBLE. OLYMPUS SUFFERED MUCH DAMAGE IN THE BATTLE....

AS *OFFICIAL ARCHITECT* OF OLYMPUS, YOU WILL LEAD THE REBUILDING AND MAKE THE CITY A *MONUMENT* THAT WILL LAST FOR ANOTHER EON.

I'LL HAVE TO START *PLANNING* RIGHT AWAY. DRAFTING PAPER, PENCILS...

PERCY JACKSON. STEP FORWARD, MY SON.

A *GREAT HERO* MUST BE REWARDED.

IS THERE ANYONE HERE WHO WOULD DENY THAT MY SON IS DESERVING?

THE COUNCIL AGREES. PERCY JACKSON, YOU WILL HAVE *ONE GIFT* FROM THE GODS. THE *GREATEST* GIFT OF ALL, ONE THAT HAS NOT BEEN BESTOWED ON A HERO IN MANY CENTURIES.

YOU SHALL BE MADE A *GOD.* IMMORTAL. *UNDYING.* TO SERVE AS YOUR FATHER'S LIEUTENANT FOR ALL TIME.

A... GOD?

NO.

NO? YOU ARE... *TURNING DOWN* THIS GENEROUS GIFT?

I'LL CHOOSE MY OWN GIFT.

FROM NOW ON, I WANT YOU ALL TO *PROPERLY RECOGNIZE* THE CHILDREN OF THE GODS.

ALL THE GODS.

THIS IS *MOST* UNPRECEDENTED.

KRONOS WOULDN'T HAVE RISEN IF IT HADN'T BEEN FOR A LOT OF DEMIGODS WHO FELT ABANDONED BY THEIR PARENTS. *LUKE* MOST OF ALL.

SO *NO MORE* UNDETERMINED CHILDREN. I WANT YOU TO PROMISE TO *CLAIM* YOUR CHILDREN BY THE TIME THEY TURN THIRTEEN. THEY'LL BE BROUGHT TO CAMP AND TRAINED TO KNOW WHO THEY ARE AND HOW TO SURVIVE.

HMPH. BEING TOLD WHAT TO DO BY A *MERE CHILD*. BUT, I SUPPOSE...

NO *UNCLAIMED DEMIGODS* WILL BE CRAMMED INTO THE HERMES CABIN ANYMORE, WONDERING WHO THEIR PARENTS ARE. THEY'LL HAVE THEIR OWN CABINS. EVEN HADES.

EVERY CHILD OF *EVERY* GOD WILL BE WELCOME AND TREATED WITH RESPECT.

ALL GODS IN FAVOR.

ALL HAIL, PERSEUS JACKSON!

HERO OF OLYMPUS! AND MY BIG BROTHER!

"SO GO DO IT."

HAPPY BIRTHDAY.

IT'S AUGUST 18TH. YOU'RE SIXTEEN, RIGHT?

YOU SAVED THE WORLD.

WE SAVED THE WORLD.

AND RACHEL IS GOING TO BE THE NEW ORACLE, WHICH MEANS SHE WON'T BE *DATING* ANYBODY.

YOU DON'T SOUND TOO DISAPPOINTED.

YOU GOT SOMETHING TO *SAY* TO ME, SEAWEED BRAIN?

RICK RIORDAN, dubbed 'storyteller of the gods' by *Publishers Weekly*, is the author of five *New York Times* number-one bestselling series with millions of copies sold throughout the world: Percy Jackson, the Heroes of Olympus and the Trials of Apollo, based on Greek and Roman mythology; the Kane Chronicles, based on Egyptian mythology; and Magnus Chase, based on Norse mythology. Millions of fans across the globe have enjoyed his fast-paced and funny quest adventures as well as his two bestselling myth collections: *Percy Jackson and the Greek Gods* and *Percy Jackson and the Greek Heroes*. Rick lives in Boston, Massachusetts, with his wife and two sons. Learn more at www.rickriordan.co.uk or follow him on Twitter @camphalfblood.

ROBERT VENDITTI is a *New York Times* bestselling author whose characters and concepts have been adapted to both film and television. He has written critically acclaimed comic-book series for Valiant Entertainment and DC Comics, as well as the graphic-novel adaptations of the worldwide best-selling series Percy Jackson, the Heroes of Olympus, and Blue Bloods. He is also the author of the award-winning Miles Taylor and the Golden Cape series for young readers. Robert lives in Atlanta, Georgia. Visit him at robertvenditti.com.

ORPHEUS COLLAR is a *New York Times* bestselling graphic novelist. He adapted, illustrated and coloured the Kane Chronicles graphic-novel series: *The Red Pyramid*, *The Throne of Fire* and *The Serpent's Shadow*. Orpheus drew layouts for *Percy Jackson and the Lightning Thief: The Graphic Novel* and coloured the Heroes of Olympus graphic novels *The Lost Hero* and *The Son of Neptune*. He also drew layouts for and coloured *Percy Jackson and the Battle of the Labyrinth: The Graphic Novel*. Orpheus lives in Los Angeles, California. Learn more at orpheusartist.com.

ANTOINE DODÉ is an award-winning illustrator, known for his graphic-novel work, including *Armelle et l'oiseau*. He studied illustration in Brussels at Saint-Luc Institute and has illustrated numerous comics and graphic novels, including the mini-series *The Crow: Curare*, written by James O'Barr. Antoine also did the pencils and inks for *Percy Jackson and the Battle of the Labyrinth: The Graphic Novel*. Learn more at antoinedode.blogspot.fr.